THE VOLCANO AWAKES!

By Julie Mitchell

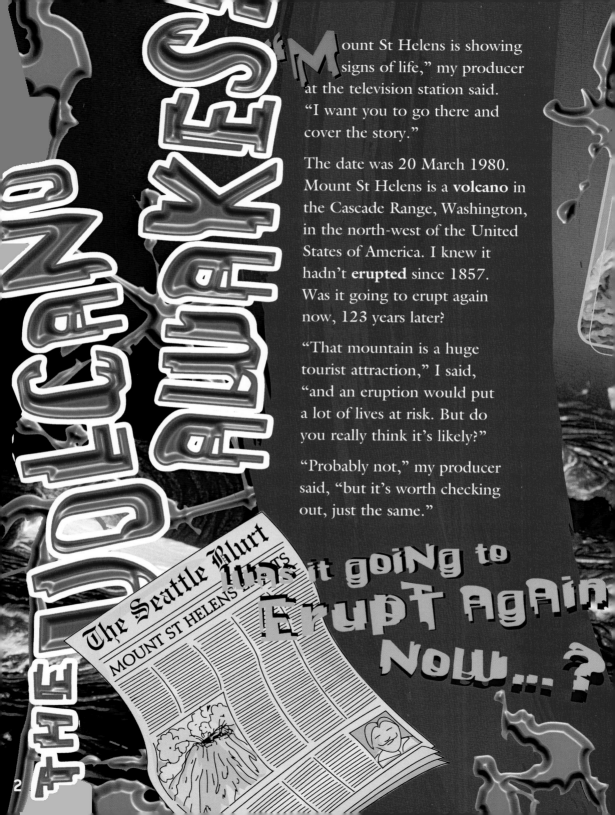

THE VOLCANO AWAKES

"Mount St Helens is showing signs of life," my producer at the television station said. "I want you to go there and cover the story."

The date was 20 March 1980. Mount St Helens is a **volcano** in the Cascade Range, Washington, in the north-west of the United States of America. I knew it hadn't **erupted** since 1857. Was it going to erupt again now, 123 years later?

"That mountain is a huge tourist attraction," I said, "and an eruption would put a lot of lives at risk. But do you really think it's likely?"

"Probably not," my producer said, "but it's worth checking out, just the same."

Was it going to erupt again now...?

The Seattle Blurt

MOUNT ST HELENS ERUPTS

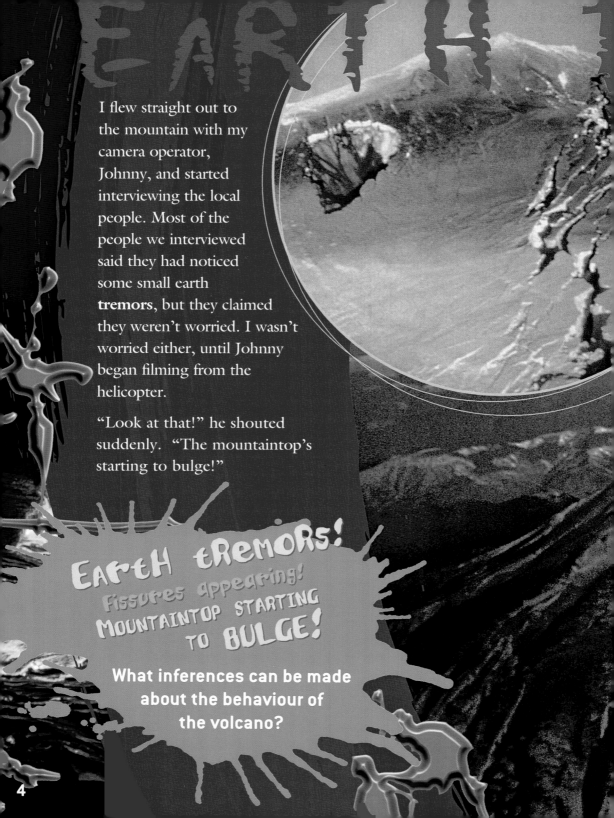

I flew straight out to the mountain with my camera operator, Johnny, and started interviewing the local people. Most of the people we interviewed said they had noticed some small earth **tremors**, but they claimed they weren't worried. I wasn't worried either, until Johnny began filming from the helicopter.

"Look at that!" he shouted suddenly. "The mountaintop's starting to bulge!"

EARTH TREMORS!
Fissures appearing!
MOUNTAINTOP STARTING
TO BULGE!

What inferences can be made about the behaviour of the volcano?

A week later, we flew over Mount St Helens again. Now there were long **fissures**, appearing in its sides. Steam was coming out of the fissures. A large **crater** opened up, blasting out more steam. Then a black cloud rolled up and dropped **ash** onto the mountainside.

Clarify
fissures

A narrow cracks
B splitting an atom
C wide craters

A, B or C?

A LARGE crater OPeNed uP...

Was a large eruption going to take place? Some of the people who lived on the mountain thought so, and they were preparing to leave.

On 10 April, a cloud of steam rose from Mount St Helens. "It must be 300 metres high!" Johnny shouted, training his camera on it.

"We're not flying any closer," our pilot said.

We were lucky that we didn't! Suddenly, the mountain began spurting streams of black rock into the air. Then it sent up dark clouds, which rained ash onto the volcano's slopes.

"The mountain's awake," Johnny said, his eyes wide with shock.

"Yes," the pilot replied. "Awake and angry."

Question:

Why would the pilot not fly any closer to the volcano? What might happen?

"The mountain's **AWAKE**"...

... "**AWAKE** and **ANGRY**."

Is this personification?

Personification — The likening of human characteristics to things and ideas.

Later, I learned that the cloud of steam was a serious warning: a major eruption was going to occur. Scientists couldn't say exactly when this would happen, but they advised everyone to leave the mountain immediately.

Over the next few days, the tourists and many of the people who lived on Mount St Helens left. But some people ignored the warning and stayed.

Question:

Why would some people ignore the warning and stay? Predict the problems they could face.

Mount St Helens was a popular tourist attraction even before the eruption.

Rescue centre in Toutle, Washington.

Rescue co-ordinators ready to give assistance.

POTENTIAL HAZARD AREA

HIGH-LOW SIRENS USED AS EVACUATION WARNING WHEN HIGH-LOW SIREN SOUNDS, EVACUATE THE AREA IMMEDIATELY

LOCAL EMERGENCY BROADCAST STATIONS (EBS)
KBAM 1270 AM
KEDO 1400 AM
KLOG 1490 AM
KLYK 105.5 FM

Warning sign on the road leading up to Mount St Helens.

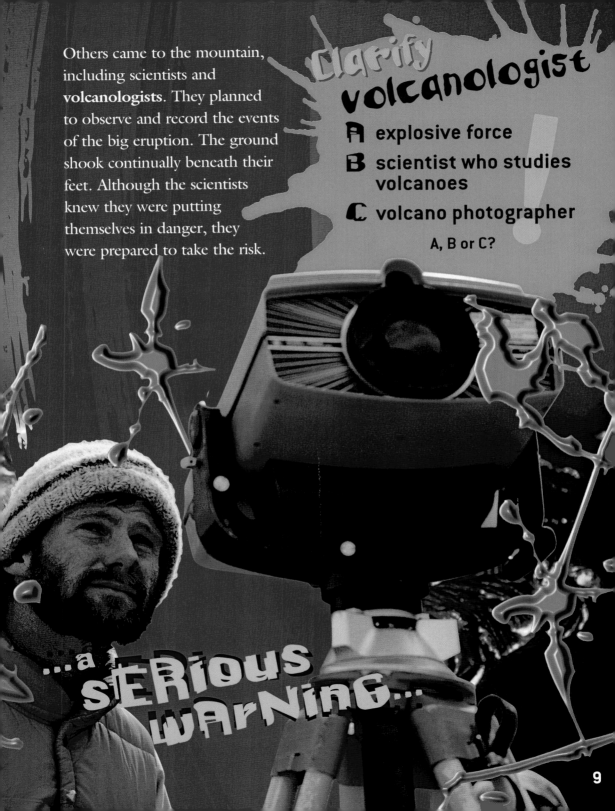

Others came to the mountain, including scientists and **volcanologists**. They planned to observe and record the events of the big eruption. The ground shook continually beneath their feet. Although the scientists knew they were putting themselves in danger, they were prepared to take the risk.

Clarify

volcanologist

A explosive force

B scientist who studies volcanoes

C volcano photographer

A, B or C?

...a SERIOUS WARNING...

... WARNING PEOPLE to LEAVE ...

By this stage, I was reporting live from the helicopter every day. And every day I expected to be covering a huge volcanic eruption. But it didn't happen.

Instead, the mountain grew quieter; it produced less steam and there were fewer tremors. The scientists continued warning people to leave, but by the end of April it looked as though there was really no reason to.

ASSIGNMENT

Find a synonym for this word!

Synonym — A word or term the same in meaning as another word or term.

I began to think the crisis might be over. Maybe the mountain had released enough pressure to settle down again. And maybe it was time I thought about asking my producer for another assignment.

REC

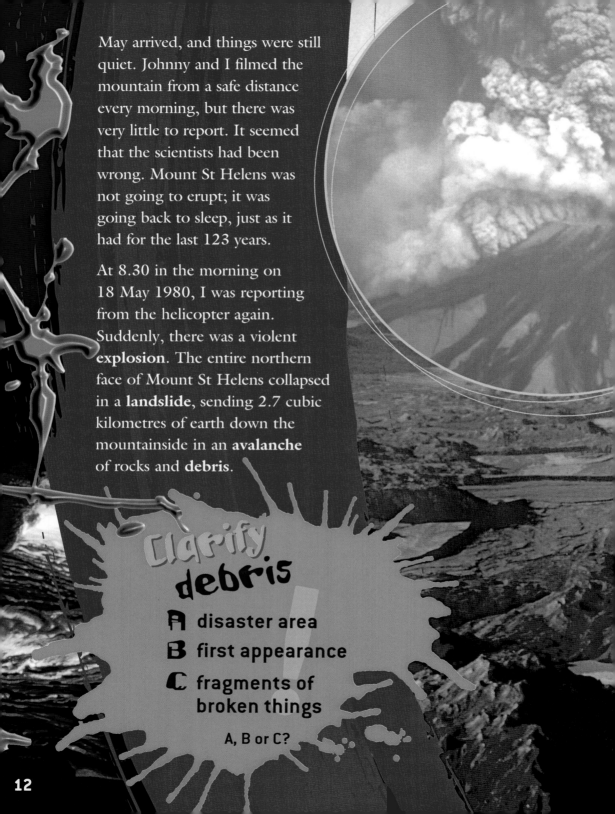

May arrived, and things were still quiet. Johnny and I filmed the mountain from a safe distance every morning, but there was very little to report. It seemed that the scientists had been wrong. Mount St Helens was not going to erupt; it was going back to sleep, just as it had for the last 123 years.

At 8.30 in the morning on 18 May 1980, I was reporting from the helicopter again. Suddenly, there was a violent **explosion**. The entire northern face of Mount St Helens collapsed in a **landslide**, sending 2.7 cubic kilometres of earth down the mountainside in an **avalanche** of rocks and **debris**.

Clarify

debris

A disaster area

B first appearance

C fragments of broken things

A, B or C?

Mount St Helens was NOT going to ERUPT. It was GOING BACK to SLEEP...

Which one is personification? Check by turning back to page 7.

...a VioLEnt EXPloSion...

13

Clouds burst into the air, one surging hundreds of metres upwards from the **peak** and another billowing out from the landslide. At the same time, a blast of air flattened all the trees near the volcano and knocked down others much further away.

"This is it!" I shouted into the microphone. "Mount St Helens is erupting!" Stunned, I looked at the mountaintop. "About 300 metres of its peak has been blasted away! The clouds of ash and steam are enormous!"

As I spoke, hot ash and rocks fell onto the slopes, starting forest fires; and **lava** swept down the mountainside. It flowed into the rivers and lakes, boiling them and sending more steam into the air.

"this is it! ... Mount St Helens is ERUPTING!"

panicky devastated
pleased
calm but scared terrified
satisfied intrigued

Which words best describe the feelings of the writer about the eruption?

At the same time, something else was happening. Water from melted **glaciers** and snow on the upper slopes was pouring down the mountainside. It combined with falling ash and the soil and rocks of the landslide, becoming a steaming **mudflow** that plunged along river valleys.

I'd seen this kind of mudflow before, and I knew it had a special name: **lahar**. Johnny and I followed its progress down the mountainside.

"It's moving at incredible speed!" I reported. "At least 60 kilometres per hour!"

"It's moving at incredible SPEED!"

TorreNt

Find an antonym for this word.

Antonym – A word that is opposite in meaning to another.

And so it was. It grew into a mighty torrent that broke the banks of rivers and carried away boulders and fallen trees. Further downstream, it destroyed roads and swept away houses.

...steaming mudflow that PLUNGed ALONG RIVeR VALLeys...

Find more examples of descriptive language.

Descriptive language – Language that paints a visual picture.

Question:

What are the major problems facing the community as a result of the disaster?

Clarify
lahar

A steaming lake

B dangerous mudflow

C steaming river

A, B or C?

The bridge DiDN'T STAND a CHANCE...

The lahar became thick with wreckage. It flowed along the Toutle River and collected a load of logs cut by forest workers. Fifty kilometres below the mountain, it pushed over full-grown trees. By the time it reached the Toutle River bridge, it was a solid moving force. The bridge didn't stand a chance; when the giant mudflow hit, it was simply shoved off its supports and carried away.

The lahar travelled on for kilometres, destroying more than 200 houses, and sweeping away thousands of hectares of forest. Finally, it spread out over the countryside, burying it in mud that was more than 100 metres deep.

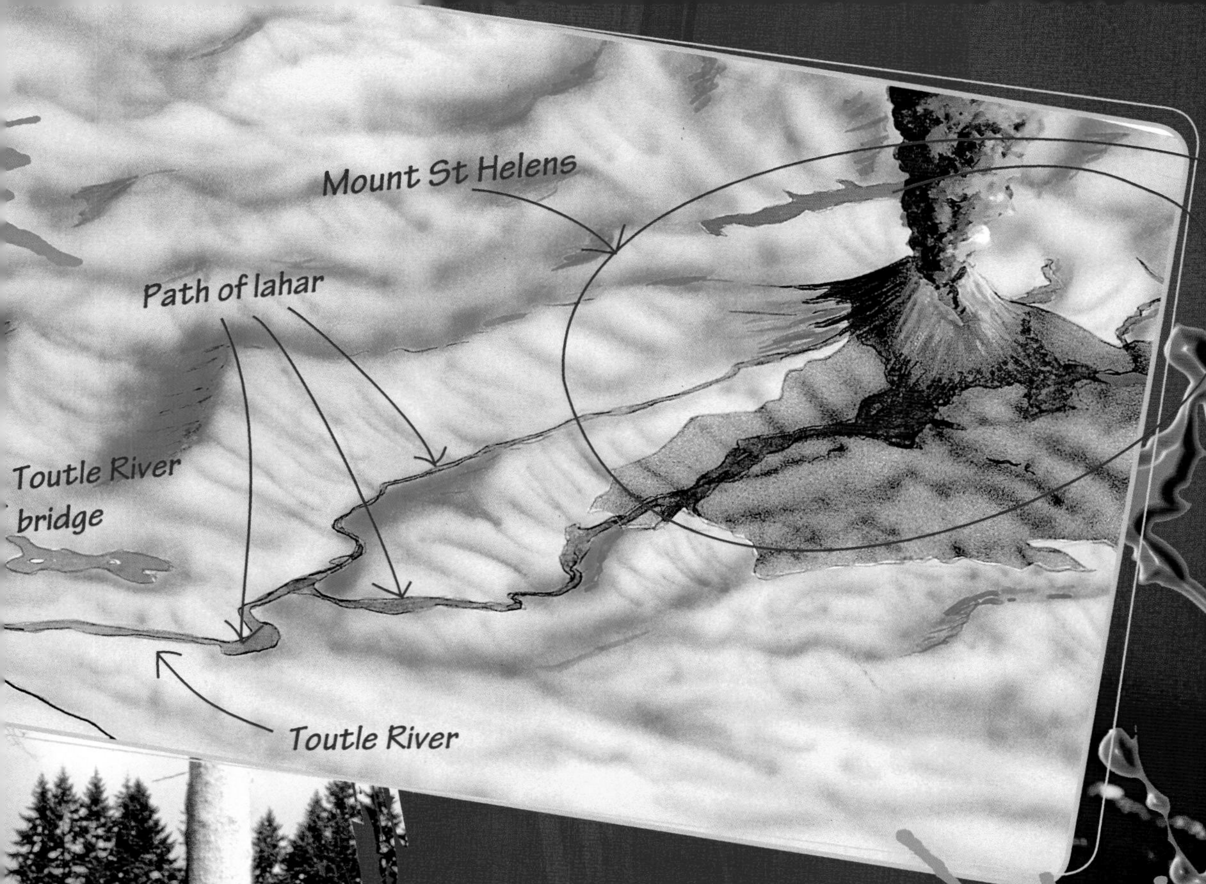

Mount St Helens

Path of lahar

Toutle River
bridge

Toutle River

Think about the language describing the flow of the lahar —

...became **THICK** with **WRECKAGE.**

...**PUSHED OVER full-grown trees.**

Find some more examples from the recount.

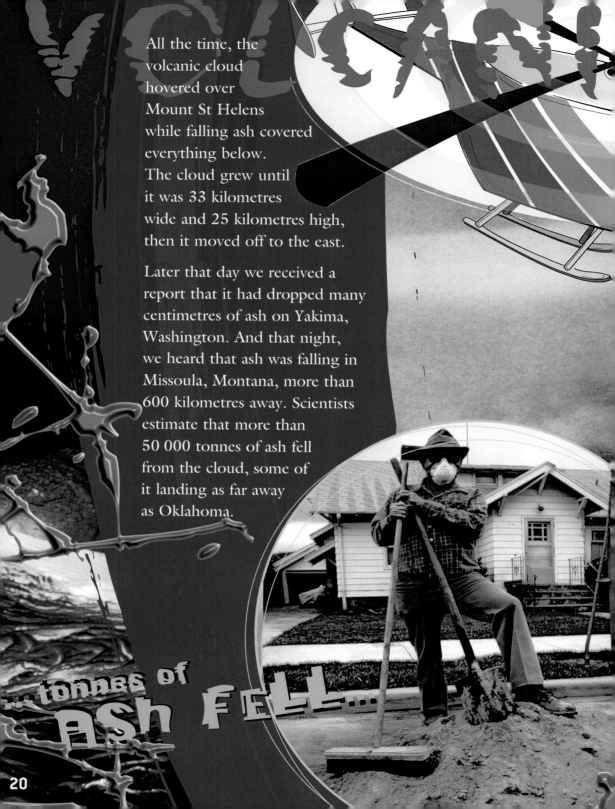

All the time, the volcanic cloud hovered over Mount St Helens while falling ash covered everything below. The cloud grew until it was 33 kilometres wide and 25 kilometres high, then it moved off to the east.

Later that day we received a report that it had dropped many centimetres of ash on Yakima, Washington. And that night, we heard that ash was falling in Missoula, Montana, more than 600 kilometres away. Scientists estimate that more than 50 000 tonnes of ash fell from the cloud, some of it landing as far away as Oklahoma.

...tonnes of ASh FELL...

Extent of ash cloud

On 20 May, two days after the eruption, Johnny and I filmed the volcano again. "It looks like a **wasteland**," Johnny said as we flew over it.

And so it did. The top of the mountain was a huge jagged crater, and everything within 20 kilometres of it was burnt. Trees, stripped of their branches, lay like scattered matchsticks on the slopes. There was no sign of animal life anywhere.

"What a terrible loss," I said. "I wonder if any of the animals sensed what was coming and got away before it happened."

"Maybe," Johnny said, "but they're homeless now."

... like SCATTERED matchsticks... Simile or metaphor?

Simile – Creates a mind picture in which one thing is said to be like another. The word *like* or *as* is used to make the comparison.

Metaphor – Creates a mind picture in which one thing is described as if it were actually that thing.

As we flew back to the TV station with our updated report, I found myself thinking about the power of the explosion which had sent more than one cubic kilometre of Mount St Helens into the air. That power was equal to the blast of 500 **atom bombs**, and had caused the deaths of several people. It was responsible for the destruction of buildings, roads, bridges, crops, forests and wildlife. And it had totally reshaped the landscape.

Could the mountain explode with such force again?

Only time will tell.

ONLY TIME WILL TELL

SUMMARY

Select the main points you would include in a summary of *The Volcano Awakes*.

- The narrator was asked by her television station to cover the Mount St Helen events.

- The mountain is a tourist attraction.

- The mountain top began to bulge and earth tremors and fissures opened up emitting steam.

- The pilot would not fly any closer.

- The mountain grew quiet again.

- May 18, 1980 a violent eruption occurred with hot ash and rocks and lava sweeping down the mountainside.

- A lahar plunged along river valleys destroying things in its path.

- Ash landed in Montana.

- The explosion left devastation and reshaped the landscape.

Weekend of fiery rioting leaves 19 dead

Oregon Journal

4-page special section

9 di... ...ost in erupti...

Monday, May 19, 1980 15¢

The Oregonian

Forecast: cloudy; high, 68; low, 50; report on Page C32

20 CENTS

FINAL STOCKS
Dow Jones up 1.62

98 persons listed as missing

Longview, Kelso face

Closing Dow Jones: 830.89 up 4.01 stocks on Page A-12

The Orego...

Mud dams lake imperil...

Mr. X picks — page 34

STREET FINAL

Oregon Journal

Thursday, May 22, 1980

'Worst thing I've ever seen'

Disaster staggers Carter

GLOSSARY

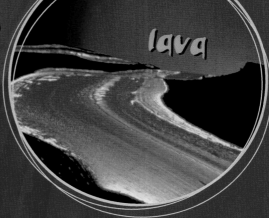

lava

ash tiny pieces of rocks and lava, like dust, that form part of an eruption

ash

atom bomb a very powerful explosive

avalanche a sudden fall of rocks, ice or snow down a mountainside

crater a round opening in the top of a volcano

debris fragments of broken rocks and other materials

erupt when a volcano forces out rock, lava and ash, usually violently

explosion a violent and destructive release of energy

fissure a narrow crack in a rock through which steam or lava can escape

glacier solid mass of ice that moves very slowly down a mountain

lahar a dangerous type of mudflow that moves rapidly down a volcano's slope

landslide a mass of rocks and soil that slides when a loosened area of a mountain gives way

lava rock that has become liquid from the heat inside the Earth

mudflow a stream of water, filled with ash, soil and rocks

peak the top of a mountain

tremor a small earthquake

volcano a mountain from which molten lava, ash, rock and gases can be hurled into the sky from beneath the Earth's surface

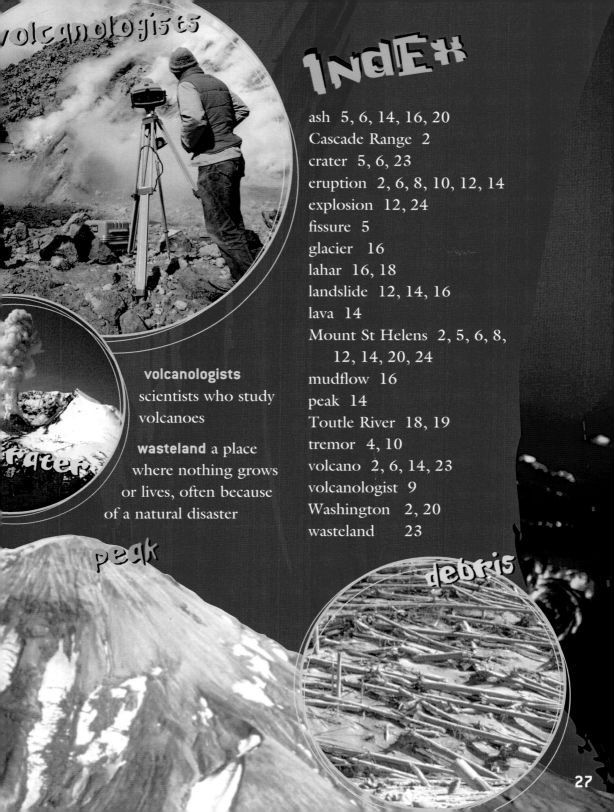

volcanologists

volcanologists
scientists who study
volcanoes

wasteland a place
where nothing grows
or lives, often because
of a natural disaster

crater

peak

debris

Think About the Text

Making connections – What connections can you make to the events and the human responses explored in *The Volcano Awakes*?

Dealing with anxiety

Dealing with evacuation and loss of home

Dealing with shock

Taking advice

Dealing with destruction

Dealing with loss of life

Following an assignment

Being in a dangerous situation

Responding to crisis

Risk taking

Text to Self

Text to Text

Talk about other informational
texts you may have read that have
similar features. Compare the texts.

Text to World

Talk about situations in the
world that might connect to
elements in the story.

Planning a Factual Recount

1
Select a real event or experience

2
Make a plan
Introduction

Who	When	Where	What

Events in order of time

Final comment

ONLY TIME WILL TELL.

3
Include personal comments
and thoughts on events
during or at the
end of a recount.

A Factual Recount...

A Uses descriptive language.

B Contains the author's personal interpretation of events.

C Uses the past tense for recording events.

D Uses the present tense for 'author talk'.

E Uses words of time to connect events, such as 'first', 'next', 'then', 'during' and 'while'.